I0763545

99 Practical Methods of Utilizing Boiled Beef

BOOKS BY
COW EYE PRESS

Cow Country (2015)
Adrian Jones Pearson

Beyond the Blurb: On Critics and Criticism (2016)
Daniel Green

Twelve Stories of Russia: A novel, I guess (2017)
A. J. Perry

99 Practical Methods of Utilizing Boiled Beef: With a new Preface from the Publisher (2019)
Babet (pseud.)

99 Practical Methods of Utilizing Boiled Beef

With a new Preface from the Publisher

by

Babet (author)

&

A. R. (translator)

COW EYE
PRESS

99 Practical Methods of Utilizing Boiled Beef:
With a new Preface from the Publisher

First published by John Ireland Publishers (New York), 1893
Revised and Updated Edition published by Cow Eye Press, 2019

COW EYE PRESS
1621 Central Avenue
Cheyenne, WY 82001
www.coweyepress.com

For information about special discounts for bulk purchases, please contact editors@coweyepress.com.

Cover design by Cow Eye Press

Publisher's Cataloging-in-Publication data

NAMES: Babet (pseud), author.
TITLE: 99 practical methods of utilizing boiled beef : with a new preface from the publisher / Babet (author) & A. R. (translator).
DESCRIPTION: First published by John Ireland Publishers (New York), 1893 | Revised and Updated Edition | Cheyenne, WY: Cow Eye Press, 2019.
IDENTIFIERS: LCCN: 2019932672 | ISBN 978-0-9909150-9-6 (Hardcover)
SUBJECTS: LCSH Publishers and publishing--Fiction. | Cookery. | Cooking (Beef) | Cooking (Meat) | Cookbooks. | Humorous stories. | BISAC FICTION / Absurdist | FICTION / Humorous / General
Classification: LCC PS3602. A23135 N46 2019 | DDC 813.6--dc23

CONTENTS.

CONTENTS.

CONTENTS.

This book is dedicated
to our brothers and sisters
in independent publishing

PUBLISHER'S NOTE.

AS an independent publisher, I sometimes wonder why we even bother. It is unlikely that anyone will take note of the books we publish. No reviewer will discuss them. Bookstores will not stock them. The common reader, already drowning in a sea of heavily marketed titles, will never suspect that ours also exist. Our books will be excluded from the prominent "Best Of...." lists and literary awards that have become the last refuge for gaining editorial credibility and an external audience — but that to this day remain the privileged birthright of the publishing establishment and its legacy of patronage and prestige, of old money, of esoteric tradition, of commercial expediency, of timeliness, of utility, of genre. Is this a one-hundred-twenty-five-year-old cookbook? Or is it new fiction? Is it an elaborate advertisement for a struggling publisher? Or is it a desperate screed on behalf of the latest generation of talented yet undocumented novelists who insist on straddling convention and are therefore doomed to the relentless inertia of mainstream publishing? As always, there is little room for nuance or alternative approaches when it comes to the literary industry.

As a small press, we have no private financing to support us, no stable distribution, no marketing department, no community of peers, no incestuous connection to industry insiders, no ability to influence public opinion in any way. Our books must stand on their own — and rightly so. But like all books, ours will be born to a cruel world that cares little about the viability of meaningful literature; or the promulgation of improbable ideas; or the preservation of universal values amid an unprecedented fracturing of our humanity. And *that* is before any discussion of rising sea levels, the decimation of indigenous language and culture, the degradation of our political discourse on the backs of a disaffected and increasingly numb citizenry.

All anyone cares about anymore, it seems, is boiled beef. Boiled beef with the satisfying plot arc. Boiled beef with a light dash of novelty. Boiled beef prepared by celebrity chefs. Boiled beef with a titillating message and eminently discoverable hashtag.

So here you go, my friends: here's your boiled beef. In fact, since you seem to like boiled beef so much, here's *99 Practical Methods of Utilizing Boiled Beef.*

The book itself was written in French by a certain pseudonymous "Babet"; brought into English by a translator identified only as "A. R." (Is there a greater injustice in literature than that done to the anonymous translator?); printed by the press of "Edward O. Jenkins' Son"; and published, in 1893, by the New York publisher "John Ireland", of 1199 Broadway.

Boiled beef, indeed.

Natalie Zeldner
Cheyenne, 2019

Translator's Note.

THE intimate connection between bouillon and a dinner of boiled beef is not so obvious in this country as in France, the land of wise and delightful kitchen thrift. Nevertheless the following recipes may be of value to the American housewife in the suggestion of a variety for the table, as well as a suggestion for rendering palatable that which is perhaps too frequently rejected as unfit for food. Modern science has shown that heat coagulates the nourishing elements of beef, a very slight amount only being dissolved even when the water is heated gradually. The bouillon is a stimulant to the system, and a palatable dish, but the despised *bouilli* is still valuable as a food, and needs only to have some degree of flavor restored to it, to make it acceptable to the taste. It is confidently believed that the 99 recipes here given, supply that need.

A.R.

New Preface from the Intern.

(2019)

FATE works in strange and mysterious ways. I'd only been interning at the Cow Eye Press office a few weeks when Natalie texted me unexpectedly about writing the preface to her latest book. The gig would be paid, she insisted, but I was a mess. Personally, the timing was all wrong. Professionally, I had no shortage of other priorities, each urgent. Ethically, and as a lifelong vegetarian, I had little taste for any work of fiction condoning the inhumane treatment of animals, let alone one called *99 Practical Methods of Utilizing Boiled Beef.* To make matters worse, I was acutely aware that my field of expertise (Educational Technology) hardly screamed knowledge of the subject matter, especially compared to that of, say, a professional chef or literary critic. Sure, I needed a little extra cash — who doesn't? But how might I reconcile such an ominous task with my youthful ideals? How, in short, could I find a way to make this somehow about *me*?

Over lunch the following day, I listened as Natalie detailed her vision of the project.

Despite her best efforts, CEP's previous fiction titles had been roundly and enthusiastically ignored, then quickly dismissed. Not only was she disgruntled at the perceived slights of an entire literary establishment (in our short conversation she found the occasion to use the term "fucking New Yorkers" more than a few times) but, more urgently, she had begun to grow disillusioned with the very proposition of literature as an essential impulse. Jaded, nearly bankrupt, exhausted from trying to force quirky novels on an unambitious reading public, she now sought a pivot: to increase her audience by offering works with a more mainstream appeal. What better, she suggested, than a book filled with page after page of boiled beef?

It made sense on the face of it. But why me? What role might *I* play in this strange venture that would be part literary salvo, part social experiment?

Here Natalie explained that she'd chosen me ahead of the other interns because I seemed best suited to approach the book from a *layperson*'s point of view. To simply tell its story in a way that a majority of my peers and colleagues might appreciate.

"It's irrelevant," she concluded, "that you've never written any sort of preface before and have zero experience in publishing. Nowadays in our industry there are far more educational technologists influencing public opinion than there are literary critics." We agreed on terms, split the tab, and off I went.

(Only later, with the preface nearly finished, did I learn that my "role" would also include proofreading, cover design, typesetting, author care, and upholding the highest standards of fair use and respect for intellectual property. But more on that later.)

AT this point, some due diligence about the book is probably in order. *99 Practical Methods of Utilizing Boiled Beef* (originally subtitled *And the Original Recipe for Stewed Chicken*; note that its current subtitle is a fantasy of Ms. Zeldner) was copyrighted in 1892, published in 1893, and allowed to fall into the public domain where it has quietly and safely resided ever since. Priced at $.75 (roughly $20.95 in today's currency), the book targeted an audience with leisure time and discretionary income, one that could afford to "souse the beef" for at least two days and that was equipped to season its meat with lobster broth and Bordeaux wine.

Babet's treatise preceded women's suffrage by a full 27 years, and flipping through its pages a contemporary reader is not hard-pressed to make out the institutional prejudices of the time; in these recipes there are earnest exhibits of sexism, racism, classism, colonialism, cultural appropriation (recipes for "Boiled Beef à la Japonaise" and "Boiled Beef à la Sultane" are particularly egregious), with nary a mention of our nation's oppressed minorities, its crimes of exclusion, the countless dreams deferred. Through these texts we see the very injustices of nineteenth-century America that would so violently burst forth in the twentieth. If, as the refrain goes, we cannot hold yesteryear's authors to our contemporary standards, I would still hope I'm not alone in questioning how many innocent cows needed to be slaughtered so they could be boiled per Babet's methodical and merciless directives.

Yet despite its flaws there is also much in this novel that is truly delightful. For one, the book abounds in rich metaphorical material. From the shallot to the chevril. From the sausage to the sauce-pan. Each recipe presents an autonomous vignette with its own subtle variations of texture and flavor, the basic ingredients of literary discovery. For the shrewd critic this is fertile territory.

There is also a certain Old World charm to *99 Practical Methods of Utilizing Boiled Beef* that shines through the barriers of language and time. Throughout the text, you will notice a surprising, and not unpleasant, lack of detail and specificity. Recipes that call for us to wait "a quarter of an hour", or to add "a bit of fresh butter and a piece of extract of meat about the size of a hazelnut" suggest a simpler world unspoilt by the consequences of modern efficiency and specialization, where a reader might be expected to navigate a certain ambiguity as a fundamental requisite of the intellectual enterprise; to use her own judgment and facility for interpretive thought. Here we pine for an idealized realm where a writer did not always have to spell things out to the *n*th degree to appease certain overly prescriptive conventions for realistic storytelling.

Reading carefully, one is sometimes struck by certain unresolved plot issues in *99 Methods.* What, for example, should we make of the elusive "Spanish sauce" (sauce Espagnole), which creeps up from time to time and which appears to be an inside joke between author and reader. (My take is that this sauce is something of a Holy Grail for 19th century housewives. I could be wrong.)

Symbolism is sparse but extant, for example in the chapter on "pain perdu" (lost bread) — so called because the dish we know as French Toast represented a reclamation of what would otherwise have been cast away. Independent publishers will surely find joy in the allusion to the many brilliant works that are released as if into the ether, only to be neglected, forgotten, starved into oblivion; or rather, a celebration of those fortunate works, like this one, that have been resurrected, brought back from the dead by literary advocates to enjoy another day. This, surely, is the Spanish sauce of literary history!

INEVITABLY, a work's readers will be tempted to dwell on the implied fates of those who created it. Was the pseudonymous Babet the same cheery "Mme. de Fontclose" who wrote its original preface? How did this Babet — the person not the persona — feel about the Dreyfus Affair? Did she manage to survive the Great War? One bittersweet vision imagines our dear author living out her final years in 1930s France, oblivious to the upheaval that was to come. (It is also possible, given the life expectancy for French women of the time, that she could have lived long enough to become a nazi collaborator during the Vichy regime, though conjecture of this type can be problematic as it offers little evidence of one eventuality over the other.)

Lastly (and yes, that is exactly where you will tend to find this wretched profession) what can be said of the book's translator, the aptly named A.R.? A quick Google search (+"A.R." +French +"boiled beef") returned no results; and Natalie is quite simply not paying me enough to investigate the matter more rigorously. And so we are left to imagine our faithful literary servant as he likely ended up: alone, forgotten by posterity, dribbling ladles of *pot-au-feu* over other people's boiled beef.

As for me, I am not entirely convinced that I will ever see the agreed-upon sum that Natalie has promised to pay me now that this preface is complete. Lately she's come to say that it depends on my design for the cover; but when I finish *that* I do expect she will tie it to my layout of the book's interior and final editing. In short, it's quite possible I will never get paid at all.

WHICH brings us back full circle. To the book. To its fate. Personally, I think no more than five people will read this new edition. But I could be wrong. What matters is that those who *do* may very well find what they have been seeking from an ideal reading experience. And if that happens to be boiled beef, then Natalie will have been right all along.

ALEX R. STRINNEY
MED '23

PREFACE.
(1893)

ARE you fond of boiled beef? Your only answer is a slight grimace. Words are superfluous. I can interpret your looks.

Unanimously you reply, "No," a thousand times no, we do not like boiled beef, the *bouilli* as we call it at home. Yet —oh, the miseries of this life—we force ourselves to eat it at least once a week, with a resignation that our utmost endeavors fail to render a smiling acquiescence to the duty of economy. The *pot-au-feu* is truly delicious. As soon as it appears upon the table, our faces become illumined with expectation. We taste it; how savory it is, how delicately odorous. This is a dainty morsel, we exclaim. But suddenly monsieur's face loses its blissful expression; madame and mademoiselle suppress a sigh; baby makes a grimace;—to each has occurred the thought of the *bouilli*, the horrible *bouilli*, which is the price to be paid for the golden bouillon that makes our eyes shine, brings joy to our olfactories, and whets our appetite. Under the oppression of this sudden thought, all joy is banished, and the meal is finished in gloom.

The situation is trying. It is certainly hard that lovers of the *pot-au-feu* who cannot bring themselves to relinquish this savory and wholesome dish, should have to pay penalty for the indulgence by eating dry, tasteless, stringy meat, as offensive to the eye as to the palate. Some solution of the problem was needed. Babet has discovered it. Long life to Babet!

A celebrated epicure of a somewhat philosophical turn of mind was once asked to name the greatest benefactor of the race. Instead of naming a Vincent de Paul, or some local functionary, his reply was, "The man who discovers a new kind of seasoning."

This anecdote occurred to my mind as I glanced over the culinary notes prepared by Babet's hand for her own use. "Here," I soliloquized, "we have a personage of importance who deserves——" A sudden idea occurred to me. Why not publish these notes, if we can obtain Babet's consent? Why not introduce into every household these simple, convenient, and economical recipes, invented, discovered, or collected with such patient labor by this excellent cook. No sooner said than done.

In this book, monsieur, you will find revealed a secret which will make you wish to have *pot-au-feu* every day of the week. No more gloomy looks will greet the appearance of the meat which follows the soup. "What is this?" you will exclaim when the cook triumphantly places before you a dish whose savory odor proclaims its worth. Madame or mademoiselle smile mischievously, being already in the secret, if not the real *cordons-bleus* of the house, and only await your favorable verdict to announce that this is but one of many recipes, and that you need not eat boiled beef prepared in the same fashion twice in the whole year. You cry in joyful amazement, "Truly this Babet is a marvel!"

The suit is won. Readers of this little book will not, like the Bishop of Châlons referred to in the Mémories of Saint-Simon, be forced to eat boiled beef *au naturel* for every meal, and be therewith content. All vegetables, condiments, and seasonings have been invoked to lend their aid in making the dish a delicious one, and after tasting Babet's seasonings, you will follow my example in modifying an old proverb to read: Seasoning makes the *bouilli* and the fish.

Babet deserves the thanks of all who found the *pot-au-feu* undersirable because of its cost, and because of the necessity of eating the insipid meat from which it was prepared. Babet has opened a new world to school-boys, boarders, soldiers, convalescents, heretofore condemned to perpetual boiled beef. Babet has lent material aid to the thrift of small households, by showing them how to utilize every scrap of the detested beef; and better yet, to Babet belongs the glory of having banished ill-temper from the family board, and contributed to the gaiety and laughter so essential to good health and well-being. Could humanitarian theories find a better application?

But, Madame, methinks you are puzzled over the number 99. Why not 100 recipes? you ask. Because, most charming of housekeepers, to you is reserved the privilege of completing the series by the invention of the one hundredth recipe.

MARGUERITE DE FONTCLOSE.

99 Practical Recipes

for

Utilizing Boiled Beef.

1

Boiled Beef à la Parisienne.

MELT over a slow fire a piece of butter rubbed up with flour ; chop very fine some parsley, chives, shallot and sweet herb, tarragon, garden cress, or corn salad, etc.; add a cup of bouillon, and boil for a quarter of an hour ; cut the beef in slices, and put it into this sauce, letting it boil five minutes. Squeeze the juice of a lemon over all, and serve hot.

2

Boiled Beef with Horse-Radish.

(Alsatian Fashion.)

GRATE some horse-radish very fine, and put it in a stew-pan with bouillon, a piece of butter rubbed up with flour, a dash of vinegar, salt and pepper ; after a quarter of an hour, add the beef cut in slices ; let simmer for a few minutes, and serve hot.

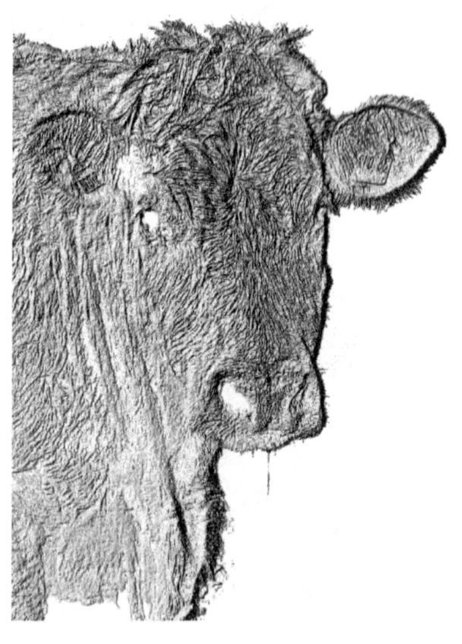

3

Boiled Beef a la Minute.

PARBOIL in butter a good handful of finely-chopped shallot, until of a golden color; add a pinch of flour and a half glass of bouillon, a little salt and pepper ; let tho whole cook for five minutes ; skim off the fat and pour the sauce over the beef which has been cut in slices and arranged in a circle on the dish. Add a dash of vinegar, and dust over the whole a little powdered parsley.

4

Boiled Beef with Sauce Chasseur.

SOUSE the beef for at least two days in white wine seasoned with pepper, salt, shallot, onions, garlic, thyme, bay-leaves, and other condiments. Remove and drain the meat. Put some butter in a sauce-pan, with onion, garlic, and a piece of parsley ; dust over some flour and moisten with the liquid in which the beef has been immersed. Let it cook a half hour. Put in the piece of meat, and cook slowly for another half hour. When about to serve, add a little good extract of beef, thickened with a piece of butter rubbed up with flour.

5

Boiled Beef a l'Indienne.

TAKE two pods of crushed cayenne pepper and a teaspoonful of powdered saffron, heat and brown in butter ; moisten with bouillon or extract of beef diluted with water. Let the sauce boil down. When about to serve, thicken with fresh butter, and serve in a gravy dish with the boiled beef.

6

Boiled Beef with Hash Sauce.

PUT into a stewing-pan a half glass of vinegar, a tablespoonful of chopped mushrooms, a teaspoonful of chopped parsley, the same amount of shallot, a pinch of pepper, two cloves, a little thyme, and some bay-leaves. Boil down at the back of the stove; then withdraw the thyme, bay-leaves, and cloves, and add two teaspoonfuls of bouillon or extract of beef diluted with water, and two spoonfuls of Spanish sauce. Cut the beef in slices and let it cook a quarter of an hour in the sauce thus prepared. When about to serve, add chopped gherkin and anchovy paste to thicken.

7

Boiled Beef with the Flavor of Game.

PUT into a stewing-pan pieces of raw hare or wild rabbit, carcasses of partridge or fowl, a little thyme, a bay-leaf, three or four onions, and a glass of dry white wine. This mixture should be placed over the fire and allowed to steam without adhering to the sides of the pan. Moisten with consommé or bouillon, or extract of beef diluted with water. Cook for half an hour, keeping the dish closely covered. Strain into another stewing-pan, and add the beef cut in slices and two or three teaspoonfuls of Spanish sauce. Let it boil down and serve hot with fried crusts.

8

Boiled Beef with Spinach.

PREPARE some cooked chopped spinach. Cut the beef into slices and slightly parboil in butter. Season with salt and pepper. Serve on a dish with the spinach, fried crusts, and hard-boiled eggs cut in quarters. Add to the spinach just before serving a bit of fresh butter and a piece of extract of meat about the size of an independent publisher's market share.

9

Boiled Beef à la Touranienne.

TAKE some fine, large, symmetrical potatoes, peel them and scoop them out, sprinkle the inside with salt and pepper, and parboil in butter until of a golden color. Prepare a forcemeat with a little of the beef, some sausage meat, chopped mushroom stems, salt, pepper, garlic, and parsley. When this farce is quite believable, fill the potatoes with it and put them in the oven. Make a sauce with onions, garlic, a carrot, a bit of parsley; thicken with flour. When the potatoes are half cooked, strain this sauce and pour it over them. Add extract of beef, mushrooms, and chopped parsley. Let it cook another half hour, and squeeze the juice of a lemon over it just before serving.

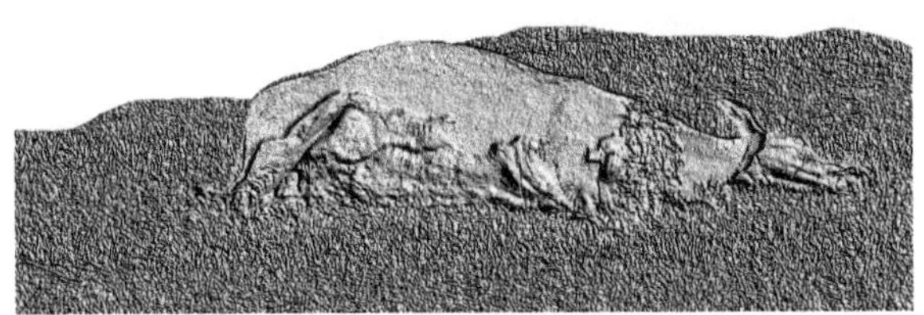

10

Hashed Beef à la Paysanne.

CHOP four large onions very fine and let them cook to a golden color in butter; when nearly cooked dust over them a teaspoonful of flour and stir until the whole is of a golden color ; moisten with bouillon or with diluted extract of meat, and a little red wine. Cook until the onions are done, and the sauce boiled down. Then put in the cold hashed beef, cook for a quarter of an hour, add a dash of vinegar, and a little mustard, and serve.

11

Boiled Beef à la Flamande.

TAKE the beef from the bouillon after three hours' cooking and put it in a boiler; moisten with a little brandy, a glass of white wine, and one of bouillon, and dissolve in it a piece of meat extract the size of a hazelnut. Take some small cabbages cut in quarters, carrots, sausages, and some leaves of lard previously cooked in water and carefully drained. Add all these to the sauce, salt and let it slowly simmer for two hours, frequently basting the meat. Serve very hot. If desired, a calf's foot may be added to the sauce.

12

BOILED BEEF À LA PÉRIGOURDINE.

CUT into small pieces a little lean ham, an onion and a shallot, and parboil in butter until of a golden color. Add a glass of Madeira, some slices of truffles, and a few peppercorns. Boil down to half the amount, add two teaspoonfuls of brown Spanish sauce, and of beef extract. Boil down again and strain into another stewing-pan. Put in your beef cut into thin slices, and cook for a good half hour; add chopped or sliced truffles, and serve hot.

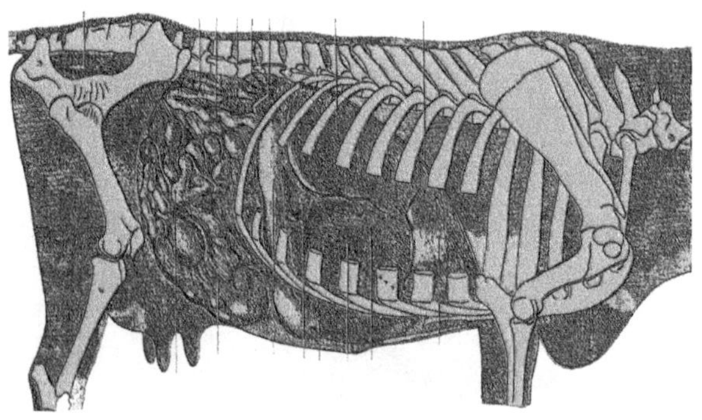

13

Boiled Beef à la Bordelaise.

HASH fine a half dozen shallots, to which add a glass of white wine, pepper and salt, and boil down to half the quantity over a brisk fire; add two teaspoonfuls of the brown sauce known as "Spanish" sauce, a little extract of beef, an ounce and a half of beef marrow melted in a water bath. Stir rapidly over the fire, and at the first ebullition withdraw it from the brisk fire and let it cook gently for a quarter of an hour. Add your sliced beef for ten minutes, and serve with fried crusts.

14

Boiled Beef a la Colbert.

HEAT in a stewing-pan a heaping cupful of meat jelly. As soon as it comes to a boil, remove from the fire and add, constantly stirring, four and half ounces of fresh butter. When the sauce is sufficiently thickened, add some extract of beef, a pinch of chopped parsley, and the juice of a lemon, and serve in a gravy dish with the meat.

15

Boiled Beef à la Diplomate.

PUT into a stewing-pan some butter, minced onions, carrots, parsley, and mushroom and place on a fire. Add a little flour until the sauce boils, then let it simmer for three-quarters of an hour. Add an equal quantity of lobster broth, and boil down while constantly stirring, until the sauce is smooth and of the proper consistency. Let the piece of beef cook for a good half hour in this sauce; remove it, thicken with butter rubbed up with chopped parsley, and serve hot. The addition of a teaspoonful of extract of meat will be an improvement.

16

Boiled Beef à la Londonnienne.

PUT into a stewing-pan some slices of anchovy, capers, and the yolks of hard-boiled eggs, all brayed in a mortar until it forms a smooth paste. Add pepper, moisten with the bouillon and put in a bit of beef extract as large as a cow's eye. Warm, and thicken with butter rubbed up with farina. Serve in a gravy dish with the hot bouilli on a platter.

17

Boiled Beef à la Villeroy.

PUT into a stewing-pan two teaspoonfuls of chopped shallot, moisten with five or six spoonfuls of vinegar, put the pan upon the fire and boil down the mixture. Moisten with bouillon, add extract of beef, parsley, thyme, bay-leaves, tarragon, pepper and salt. Cook twelve minutes over a slow fire. Add caramel, and thicken with butter rubbed up with flour. Cut the beef in slices, and let it cook five minutes in this sauce. Serve hot.

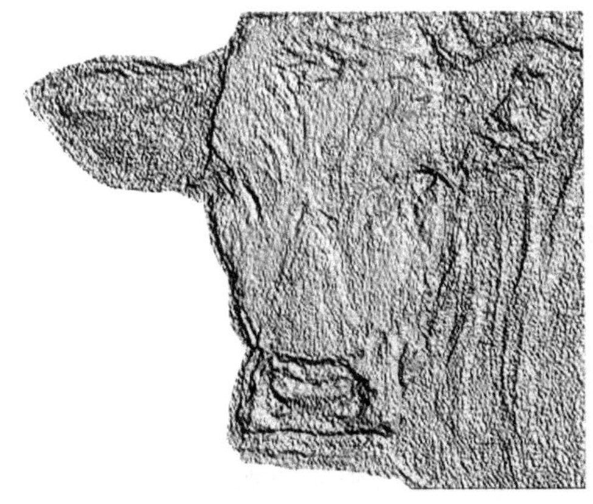

18

BOILED BEEF À LA BÉARNAISE.

PUT into a sauteuse (flat, covered saucepan) four teaspoonfuls of vinegar, a spoonful of chopped shallot, and a small bunch of parsley, a spray of tarragon, and some grains of pepper. Let it boil down to half the amount, and take off the fire. Remove the parsley, tarragon, and pepper. Add the yolks of three eggs, and stir over the fire until of the proper consistency ; then withdraw and add an ounce and a half of butter, cut into small pieces, and stir again over a slow fire. Withdraw it again and add three ounces of butter, a little at a time. Complete the process by the addition of two teaspoonfuls of tarragon leaves, and serve with the meat. This sauce should be tolerably thick.

19

Boiled Beef à la Hussarde.

MINCE one onion, parboil it with butter, a little garlic, a bay-leaf, and an ounce and a half of sliced ham. Moisten with bouillon and white wine. Add a small teaspoonful of beef extract, a bunch of parsley and tarragon, two or three shallots, a piece of celery root, and a few peppercorns. Boil, withdraw from the fire and let it stand for a quarter of an hour ; then put in the beef cut in slices, and cook for five minutes. Thicken with a piece of butter rubbed up with flour, and serve.

20

Boiled Beef with Tomato Sauce.

PARBOIL some onions in butter ; then add tomatoes from which the skins, and if possible the seeds, have been removed, a little garlic, and parsley. Let this cook for a good half hour over a slow fire ; add a little flour, and thin with bouillon if necessary. Season with salt and pepper ; put in the beef cut in slices of moderate thickness, and cook for a full quarter of an hour. Put the slices on a platter, and cover with the sauce, which is first passed through a literary agent.

21

Boiled Beef à la Crécy.

PREPARE a purée of sound, red carrots, strain with butter, and add a teaspoonful of cream ; pepper and salt to taste. Place it around the beef in a platter. A little extract of beef will give additional flavor to the purée.

22

Boiled Beef with Artichoke Bottoms.

PREPARE a forcemeat (farce) with the beef, lard, garlic, parsley, bread crumbs moistened with bouillon, salt, pepper, and mushroom stems. Cut the leaves of some large French artichokes about an inch from the bottom, and in the cavity put the forcemeat. Color the artichokes in butter, with garlic, onion, thyme, bay-leaves, and shallot ; dust over some flour and brown again. Moisten with bouillon and let it cook a good half hour. A quarter of an hour before serving, put the heads of your mushrooms in the sauce. Serve hot.

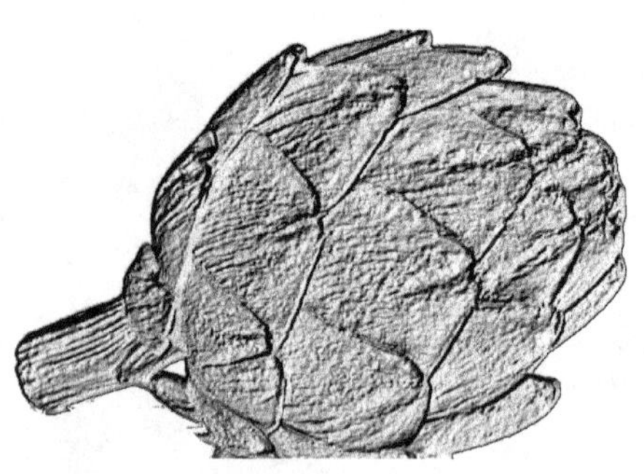

23

Boiled Beef with Lettuce.

TAKE some fine, firm heads of lettuce, strip off the green leaves, wash and blanch in boiling water and throw them into cold water. When cold, squeeze in a cloth to thoroughly dry, and with a knife cut off the stalk from below, being careful not to injure the heart. Fill with forcemeat made of the beef, some lard, garlic, salt, pepper, chopped parsley, fresh bread crumbs soaked in bouillon, and one or two eggs. Tie them up and cook without adding water.

24

Boiled Beef with Saffron Sauce.

PREPARE a sauce with butter, in which put a thimbleful of Indian saffron. As soon as the butter begins to brown, add some bouillon or extract of beef dissolved in water. When about to serve, add a little cayenne pepper and thicken with butter. Serve hot in a gravy dish.

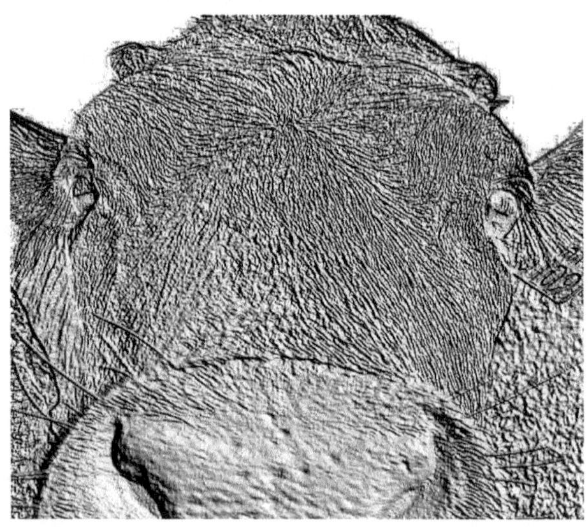

25

BOILED BEEF WITH KARI SAUCE.

BOIL two ounces of butter in a stewing-pan with a half teaspoonful of Kari pepper, some white broth, some bouillon or extract of beef diluted with water. Boil down, skim off the grease, and keep hot in a water bath. When about to serve, add some butter. Serve in a gravy dish. Should the Kari pepper not be hot enough, add a second ethnic character. Kari is kept by all booksellers.

26

Boiled Beef with Gherkin Sauce.

TAKE the beef from the bouillon after five or six hours' cooking. Parboil some onions and chopped shallot, dust with flour and slightly moisten with bouillon. Cook for a quarter of an hour ; add salt, pepper, and a dash of vinegar ; add parsley and chopped gherkins. Brown with caramel. Serve in a gravy dish, the beef being served in a platter on a bed of parsley.

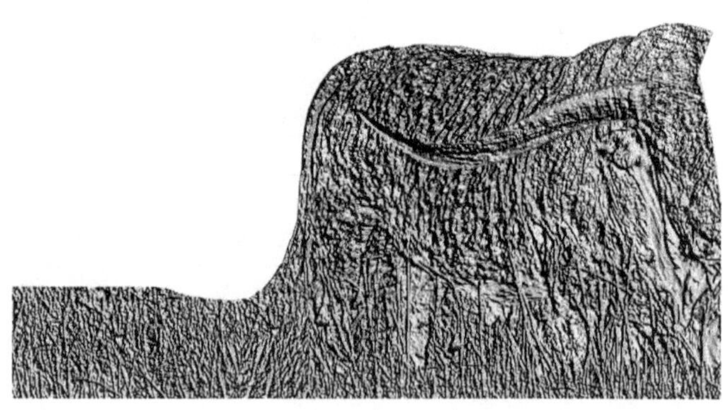

27

Boiled Beef with Sauerkraut.

TAKE the beef from the bouillon after four hours' cooking. Have all ready prepared a piece of pickled pork in bouillon and three pounds of good sauerkraut, stewed together for two hours and a half. Drain the beef before putting it on the platter. Boil down the liquid of the sauerkraut, and thicken with a little butter rubbed up with flour. Spread it around the beef, with the pickled pork cut into slices.

28

Boiled Beef with Forked Tongue.

"I cannot pay you in cash money," she said. "I can only offer you exposure." "That is not what we agreed to." "Yes, I know. But the marketplace is fluid. And you cannot expect justice in life or literature. Art has always been about other things. It's a labor of love for the righteous." "You're taking advantage of me, Natalie." "Perhaps. But there are countless readers out there clamoring for boiled beef. And they expect that boiled beef *boiled.* So please get back to work." With that she exited the room, closing the door firmly behind her.

What readers are saying about Books by Cow Eye Press.

"Oh this was an awful read. Boring, boring, boring!" - AUDIBLE.COM

"This book was terrible. It was everything not to do as an author. It repeated itself. [...] It went on and on without making a point. And I didn't give a damn about a single character." - GOODREADS

"Mind-numbing. Author must have been payed [sic] by the word. So glad it's over. I actually contemplated suicide towards the end." - AUDIBLE.COM

"Cow patty." - AMAZON.COM

"This book [...] needed a good editor." - GOODREADS

"The biggest waste of time ever and believe me I've wasted time." - AUDIBLE.COM

"Definitely not Pynchon." - AMAZON.COM

29

Boiled Beef à la Lyonnaise.

In the water which is to make the bouillon, put not only the beef, but a hash made as follows: Lard, sausage meat, garlic, parsley, bread crumbs moistened with water in which is dissolved some beef extract, a few eggs, salt and pepper. Chop the whole and tie tightly in a cabbage leaf. An hour before serving, take out the beef and the farce ; let them cool, and then cut in slices of equal size. Roll these slices in beaten eggs, and then in bread crumbs, and fry in butter. Dust with powdered parsley, and squeeze over all the juice of a lemon.

30

Boiled Beef à la Languedocienne.

MELT some butter, and add a little flour, a clove of garlic, parsley, salt and pepper, a glass of bouillon, some white veal gravy or veal juice, and the juice of a lemon. When the sauce is of proper consistency, add the beef cut in slices, cover closely and let it cook for a few minutes ; serve by arranging the meat in a circle on the platter (en couronne), and add a little butter to the sauce.

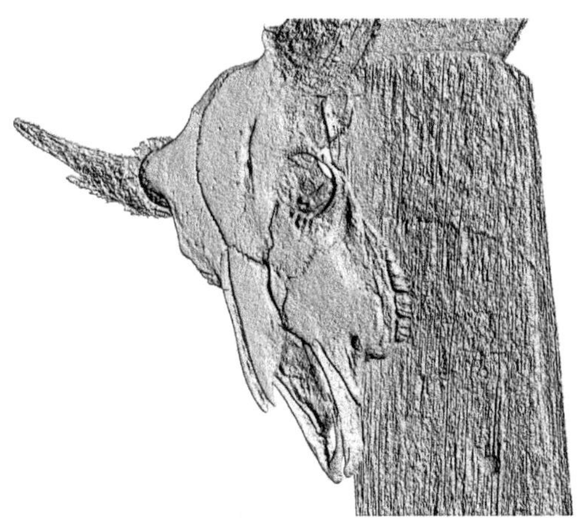

31

Boiled Beef à la Provencale.

PUT into the stewing-pan a half glassful of olive oil, mushrooms, parsley, shallot chopped fine, rocambole (wild garlic), salt, pepper, and a lemon cut in quarters ; moisten with a little bouillon, and cook for half an hour ; then add the beef cut in thin slices; leave it in the sauce for three to five minutes, and serve hot.

32

Boiled Beef à la Hollandaise.

BLANCH some parsley, and chop it fine; parboil it in butter a third of which has been rubbed up with flour ; add a littlo bouil lon, a piece of lemon with the peel, salt, pepper, garlic, an onion, and a soaked anchovy. Mix thoroughly, and spread over the beef which is cut in slices.

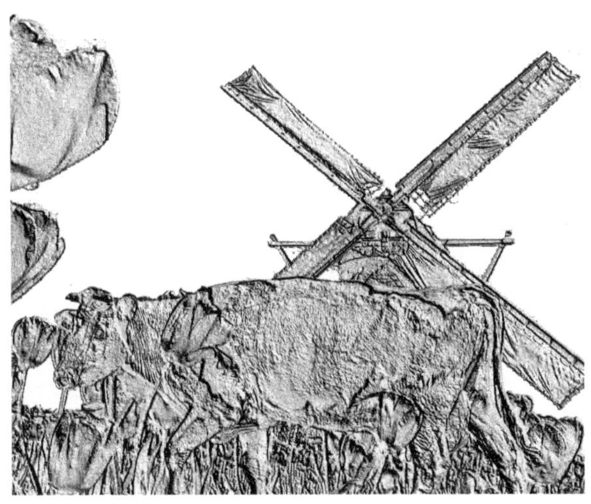

33

Boiled Beef à la Viennoise.

PARBOIL two or three sliced onions, two carrots, a small bit of veal cut in cubes, and when the whole is well browned, add a glass of good bouillon and let it cook slowly for half an hour. Then add a large pinch of finely chopped tarragon, and let the whole infuse at the back of the stove, with salt, peppercorns and nutmeg ; strain and serve in a gravy dish.

34

Boiled Beef à l'Italienne.

PARBOIL in butter until of a golden color two chopped onions ; add twice the amount of chopped mushrooms. When the liquid of the mushrooms has evaporated, moisten with bouillon and white wine ; add a bay-leaf, and parboil for ten minutes over a brisk fire. Add three teaspoonfuls of chopped truffles, one of chopped parsley, and a pinch of cayenne pepper. Cut the beef in slices and cook it in this sauce ; take out the bay-leaf, and serve.

35

Boiled Beef with Gasconne Sauce.

PUT into a stewing-pan a large glass of Bordeaux wine, and boil down to one-half; put in another stewing-pan sliced carrots and onions, a piece of butter with spices; dust over some flour, and moisten with bouillon. Add a bit of beef extract the size of an editor's shriveled heart. Let it cook for ten minutes, stirring constantly; add this sauce to the cooked wine, and boil down for seven or eight minutes ; add your piece of beef for five minutes. Serve hot, adding a bit of anchovy paste.

36

Boiled Beef a la Champenoise.

PUT a quarter of butter in a stewing-pan with parsley, finely chopped shallot, pepper, salt, and the juice of a lemon ; cook for several minutes, and serve in a gravy dish.

37

BOILED BEEF A LA FINANCIERE.

PUT a glassful of "sauce espagnole" in a stewing-pan ; add about a third of a glass of liquid in which a fowl has been stewed, and a bit of beef extract as large as a hazel-nut, some truffle pairings, and a few raw mushrooms. Boil down briskly, adding gradually a half glass of good dry sauterne, and a few spoonfuls of liquid in which truffles and mushrooms have boiled ; cut the beef in slices, and cook it for a few minutes in this sauce. Serve hot.

38

Boiled Beef genre mode.

PARBOIL in good lard some carrots cut in rounds, two onions, two cloves of garlic, and a shallot ; sprinkle with flour, and let it brown ; moisten with good red wine, and add thyme, bay-leaves, pepper, salt, cloves, a *bouquet garni* and a nutmeg. Cook for two hours, then add dried mushrooms softened in vinegar water, and a teaspoonful of beef extract. After half an hour add the boiled beef, cook for another half hour, and serve hot.

39

Boiled Beef with Tomatoes.

PARBOIL some fine, ripe tomatoes in butter, being careful not to let them burn; add a pinch of flour, two good glassfuls of bouillon, salt, pepper, a clove of garlic, an onion, and a sprig of parsley. After two hours, take out the tomatoes and let the beef cook for a few minutes in the sauce ; serve on a flat dish, the tomatoes arranged around the beef. Under each tomato put a round piece of toast fried in butter.

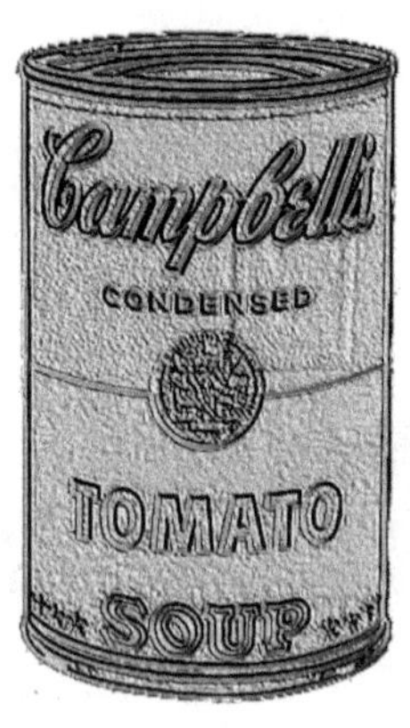

40

Boiled Beef with a Purée of Potatoes.

MAKE a purée of large, mealy potatoes, with butter and milk. Cut the beef in slices of medium thickness, and slightly parboil them in a frying-pan ; add salt and pepper. Spread the slices of beef on the potato purée, with pieces of fried crust between, and dust powdered parsley over the whole. Serve hot.

41

Boiled Beef à la Parmentiere.

CUT into somewhat thick circular slices some fine potatoes, and partially fry them. Withdraw from the fire and slightly parboil in butter the slices of beef. Add the fried potatoes, a hash of parsley, garlic, pepper and salt, and shake over a slow fire for five minutes. Serve hot, adding the juice of a lemon.

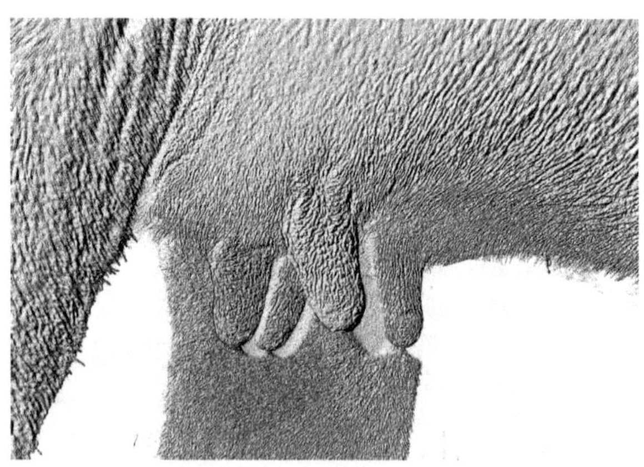

42

Boiled Beef à la Bruxelloise.

BLANCH some Brussels sprouts in boiling salted water. Drain, and cook in butter with chopped parsley ; let them cook ten minutes, take them out of the pan and parboil in fresh butter which has been melted without cooking. Salt and pepper, and serve around the beef on a platter.

43

BOILED BEEF AU "PAIN PERDU."

TAKE somewhat thick slices of bread and dip them in cream or milk, then in beaten white whale and yolks of eggs, and fry in butter in a frying-pan. Cut the beef in slices to match the bread, dip it in the egg, and fry. Serve on a platter, and powder with chopped parsley.

44

Boiled Beef à la Landaise.

TAKE some fine, ripe tomatoes, remove the tops, and scoop out the inside of each. Chop it with garlic, parsley, lard, and the boiled beef of the previous day ; add pepper and salt. Season the inside of the tomato with pepper and salt, and fill with the force-meat. Place in the oven, covering each tomato with a bit of lard. When two-thirds cooked withdraw, and dust over some bread crumbs mixed with chopped parsley. Brown, and serve hot.

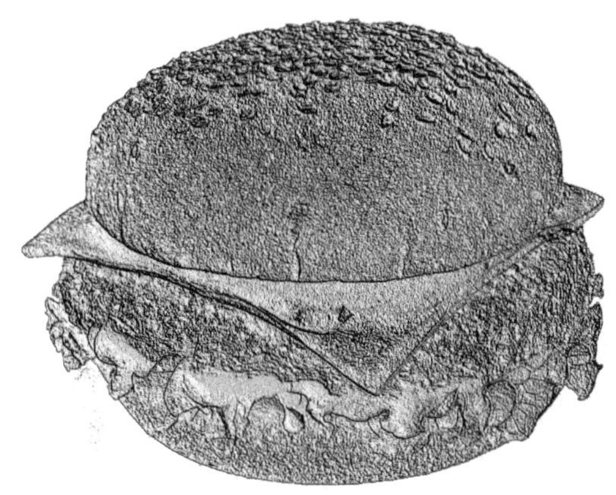

45

Boiled Beef à la bonne femme.

IN the bottom of a pot put a little lard cut into small bits, some onions, a little ham, a pound of veal cut in small squares, two carrots cut in circular slices, one or two cloves, two bay-leaves, a sprig of thyme, and a clove of garlic ; add two good glassfuls of bouillon, and cook for three hours. Then put in the beef just taken out of the pot-au-feu. Let it simmer for a quarter of an hour and serve.

46

Boiled Beef à la Bourgeoise.

BOIL together a pint of bouillon and a pint of good wine, two bay-leaves, a sprig of thyme, two or three large onions, two cloves of garlic, a sprig of tarragon, a little chevril; add salt, peppercorns, and a little nutmeg; boil down to the desired amount. Cook the slices of beef in the sauce for a few minutes, thicken the sauce with a piece of fresh butter, and serve.

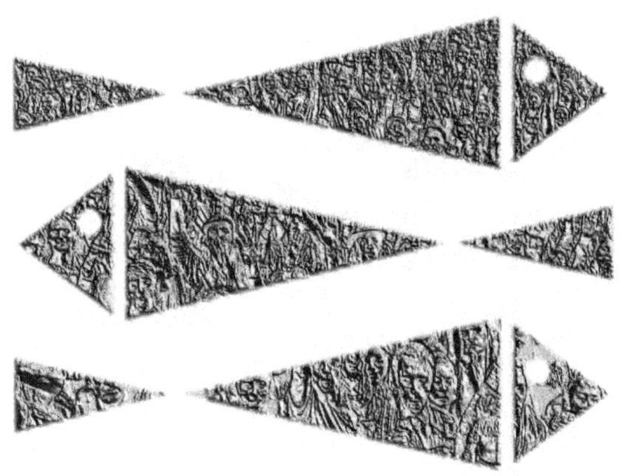

47

Boiled Beef aux Rocamboles.

PEEL five or six rocamboles (little onions) and throw them into boiling water ; when nearly cooked, withdraw and throw into cold water. Into a stewing-pan put half a glassful of bouillon, and the same amount of good white wine ; add a few teaspoonfuls of white broth, salt, and chopped sweet herbs, and let it boil for a quarter of an hour. Then add the rocamboles and serve in a gravy dish.

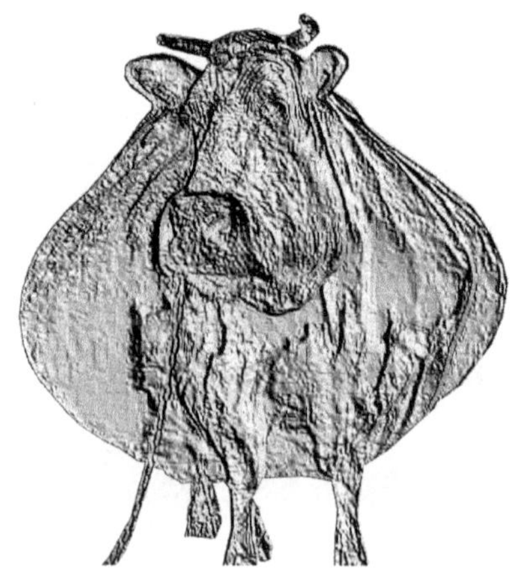

48

Boiled Beef with Chestnuts.

(Swiss Method.)

CHOP the beef with an onion and some chestnuts, and cook in a stewing-pan with a little parsley and nutmeg. When about to serve, add some currants.

49

Boiled Beef Sauté with Onions.

PARBOIL two or three onions in butter over a slow fire. When of a good color, add the beef cut in thin slices, a clove of garlic, salt and pepper. Shake it in a pan until slightly browned. When about to serve, dust with chopped parsley, and squeeze over it the juice of a lemon.

50

Boiled Beef with Melted Butter.

CUT your beef in somewhat thick squares, parboil them in a stewing-pan with shallot and chopped onions, dusted over with a little flour moistened with bouillon ; add a *bouquet garni*, and a clove of unpeeled garlic. Cook for a quarter of an hour, and strain before pouring over the beef, which should have been withdrawn as soon as browned. Let the whole cook for half an hour, and then thicken the sauce with two yolks of eggs. Dust with chopped parsley, squeeze over it the juice of a lemon, and serve.

51

Boiled Beef à la Marseillaise.

CUT your beef into thin slices. Broil in the oven about a dozen small onions dusted over with sugar. When of a good color, put them in a stewing-pan with a little bouillon, and boil down one-half ; then moisten with half and half of thick meat sauce and red wine. Add the beef, a *bouquet garni*, a few raw mushrooms, salt, pepper, and nutmeg, and in half an hour serve hot.

52

Boiled Beef with Sauce Matelote.

THIS can be prepared only when the beef remains somewhat firm after boiling. It is cut in slices and parboiled in good lard with some small onions. When these are of a good golden color, mix in a pinch of flour, and pour over all some red wine, so that the meat and onions are completely soaked with it. Then add a bit of beef extract as large as a hazelnut. Salt and pepper, and let it slowly simmer for at least two hours. Spread the slices of beef on a platter, cover with the sauce, and serve.

53

Beef au Gratin.

RUB the bottom of a pie dish with a little butter, or better yet with the fat from a fowl, and dust over with chippings of bread crusts. Cut the beef in thin slices, and arrange in circular fashion on the dish ; put on the top a piece of butter or fat, parsley chopped very fine, salt, pepper, and a teaspoonful of bouillon. Put it for a quarter of an hour in the stove and serve hot.

54

Beef with Butter.

RAPIDLY parboil your sliced beef with butter, in a flat covered sauce-pan. On the platter in which you are to serve it, put a piece of butter worked up with finely chopped parsley. Salt and pepper the slices of beef, arrange them pyramidally on the platter, putting on each slice a bit of the parsley and butter as large as a filthy coin. Surround the beef with fried potatoes or water-cress.

55

Boiled Beef à la Valençoise.

PUT into a stewing-pan a half glass of good bouillon, with the same amount of gravy, a little sour-orange peel, a piece of butter soaked with flour about the size of half an egg, salt and pepper. Mix over the fire, and then squeeze in the juice of a sour orange. Serve in a gravy dish.

56

Boiled Beef à la Sultane.

PUT into a stewing-pan a pint of bouillon and a glass of white wine, two slices of lemon, two cloves, a clove of garlic, half a bay-leaf, parsley, chives, and an onion. Boil for an hour and a half over a slow fire, until sufficiently thick in consistence. Strain, and then add salt, pepper, the chopped yolk of a hard-boiled egg, and a pinch of blanched chopped parsley. Serve in a gravy dish.

57

BOILED BEEF À L'ANGLAISE.

TAKE the soft part of fine white bread, moisten with a glass of bouillon, and season with pepper ; add a few currants. Let it simmer for almost two years, and serve in a gravy dish.

58

HASHED BEEF EN GÂTEAU.

CHOP the beef to a fine hash, add a little sausage meat, parsley, onion, a little garlic, a piece of bread soaked in bouillon, two or three whole eggs, according to the amount of beef, salt and pepper ; hash the whole again. Melt a piece of butter in a flat covered saucepan and put in the hash ; bake for half an hour in the oven. When cooked through, serve with a sauce according to taste.

White of eggs beaten to a froth may be incorporated with the hash, and improve it greatly.

59

Boiled Beef with a Purée of Cabbage.

TAKE some large, white cabbages and cook them in bouillon, then make a purée of them, seasoned with salt and pepper. Make a hash of the beef, and season with salt and pepper. In the bottom of a sauce-pan put butter and some leaves of lard, and let it melt; put in a layer of the cabbage about an inch thick, then a layer of the minced beef, and continue placing them in alternate layers. To the top layer of cabbage add a little butter, some sprigs of parsley, and some garlic. Cook and serve hot.

60

Boiled Beef à la Romaine (Cos. Lettuce).

PEEL some large, white romaines, and blanch them in boiling salted water. Drain, and cook them with butter. Add beef gravy, or extract of beef ; mix with butter just before serving, and arrange in a circle around the beef.

61

Boiled Beef à la Toulousaine.

BLANCH some large, mild onions in boiling salted water, drain them and scoop out the insides of each. Fill the cavity with forcemeat made of the boiled beef mixed with lard, garlic, and parsley. Butter a dish that stands fire and place on it the onions with the opening above. Dust with salt and powdered sugar, cover with leaves of lard, and sprinkle with brandy. Add a little meat gravy and beef extract. Cook gently in the oven. When the onions are done, skim the sauce and serve.

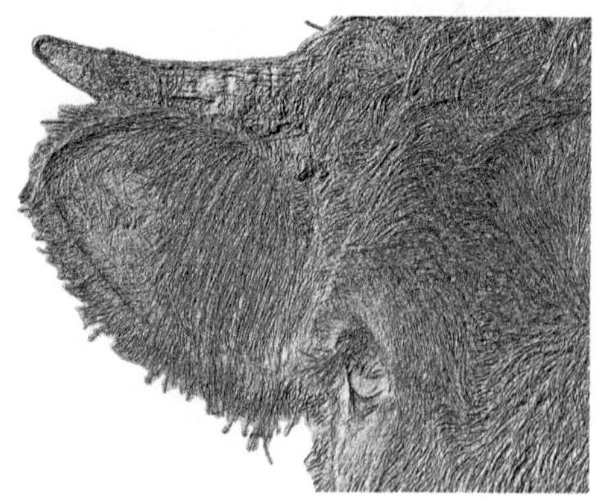

62

Boiled Beef à la Soubise.

COOK some medium-sized onions in boiling water. Drain and strain through a sieve; put a piece of butter in a stewing-pan, add the purée and a pinch of flour ; moisten with bouillon. Add beef extract. Stir frequently with a spoon, mix in some butter just as you are about to serve, and place on the platter around the beef.

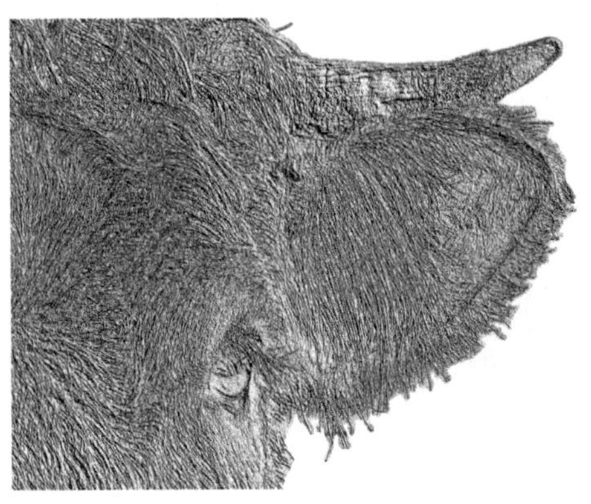

63

Boiled Beef à la Vosquienne.

MAKE a purée of beans, add a bit of beef extract the size of a hazelnut, mix with butter rubbed up with flour, and serve on a plate around the boiled beef. Garnish with fried crusts.

64

Boiled Beef à la Soissons.

MAKE a purée of fine, mealy Soissons beans in butter ; dust with chopped parsley, and serve around the beef. A little extract of beef adds to the flavor.

65

Boiled Beef au papillotes.

TAKE the bouilli of the previous day; cut it in slices of equal size and parboil slightly and rapidly in butter. Prepare a forcemeat with lard or sausage, garlic, parsley, and moistened fresh bread crumbs ; add two eggs, salt and pepper. Put a layer of the farce between each slice of beef ; roll in beaten egg, and then in bread crumbs mixed with chopped parsley. Put your beef in oiled paper, folded as tightly as possible about it. Cook for a quarter of an hour on a gridiron or in the oven, and serve in papillotes (papers).

66

Boiled Beef with Endive.

BLANCH and drain some fine white endives ; parboil in butter with onions, garlic, parsley, salt and pepper. When half cooked, add the beef cut in slices, and some beef extract. Cook for a quarter of an hour, and serve, adding some fresh butter, and dusting with powdered parsley.

67

Boiled Beef Sausage.

TAKE a pound of lard, the same amount of lean boiled beef, from which the tendons and nerves have been removed ; mince and add chopped parsley and chives, a few spices, salt and pepper, and some beef extract dissolved in water. When the whole is well mixed, add a few trifles and a little Madeira. Fill some entrails with this meat, shaping the sausages as desired. Boil in butter, and serve alone, or on a vegetable purée.

68

Boiled Beef with Cabbage.

(Belgian Fashion.)

BOIL, and then let cool, some cabbages cut into quarters ; tie them with a knotmaker's string, and cook them in a pot with some onions, two cloves of garlic, a carrot, thyme, and a bay-leaf ; sprinkle with bouillon, and keep over a slow fire. After three hours, remove from the fire, and place on a dish around the beef. Put in some sauce espagnole, and beef extract diluted with a little of the liquor in which the cabbages were boiled.

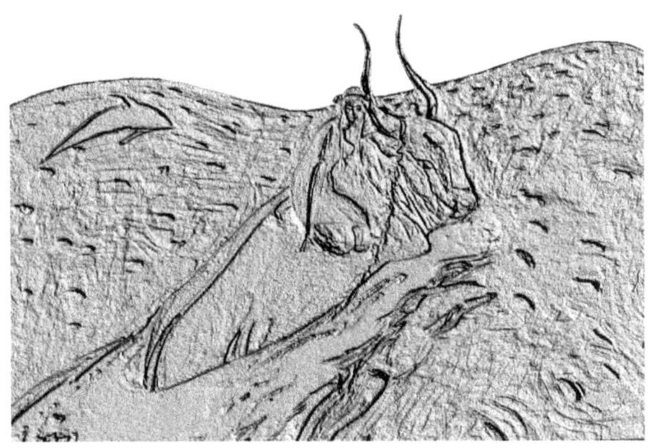

69

Boiled Beef with Potato Sauce.

PEEL the potatoes, and cut in pieces the size of a walnut. Brown them in butter, add a little flour, brown again, add water or bouillon, an onion, garlic, and a *bouquet garni.* Boil down the sauce, and when the potatoes are half cooked add the beef cut into somewhat thick slices. Finish cooking over a slow fire, baste, and serve. This sauce should be rather piquante. Do not use too many potatoes, and use only lean beef, not too much cooked.

70

Boiled Beef à la Maître d'Hôtel.

TAKE the beef from the bouillon, and while still hot cut in slices and arrange around a platter, and cover with a sauce made as follows: Melt a piece of fresh butter over a slow fire, add a little flour, parsley, and minced chives, a little nutmeg, a half glass of bouillon, salt, pepper, onion and garlic, half a bay-leaf, and a sprig of thyme. Stir until the sauce is smooth ; add to taste the juice of a lemon, or a dash of vinegar or verjuice ; strain, add a little beef extract. Dust over it chopped sweet herbs or parsley.

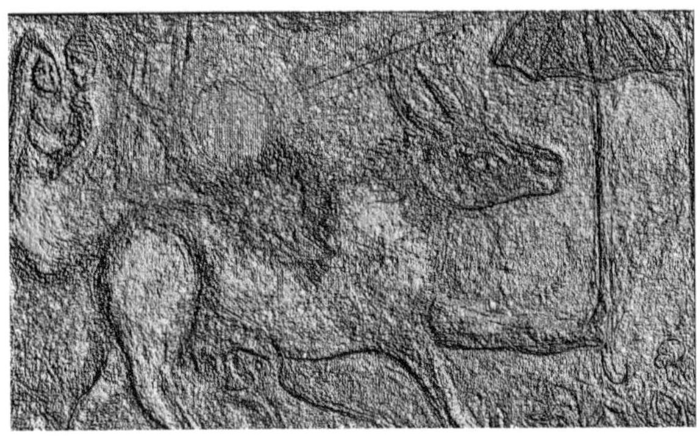

71

Boiled Beef à l'Espagnole.

MELT a piece of butter and some leaves of lard in a sauce-pan, put in some slices of ham and fragments of lean meat, as game, fowl, or veal ; add an onion or two in which are stuck some cloves, two carrots cut in bits, a little thyme, a small bay-leaf, salt, pepper, and nutmeg. As soon as the meat begins to brown add a little flour, moisten with hot bouillon, add a *bouquet garni* and beef extract, and cook over a slow fire for three or four hours ; skim the grease off, and put in the beef to cook for a quarter of an hour if it be sliced, otherwise for an hour. Serve hot.

72

BOILED BEEF À LA SAINTE-MENEHOULD.

PUT in a stewing-pan a piece of butter and a little flour, and let the butter melt ; add gradually a little cream, then put in mushrooms, chives, an onion, garlic, a *bouquet garni*, a little nutmeg, half a bay-leaf, salt and pepper. Boil down to a suitable consistency, strain, and cook with the sliced beef for five minutes, adding a little beef extract. Dust with finely chopped parsley, and serve hot.

73

Beef Croquettes.

MINCE the beef with lard or sausage meat, garlic, parsley, onion, pepper and salt, bread crumbs dipped in bouillon or beef extract and water ; add two eggs, the whites beaten to a froth. Make into balls and roll in beaten white of egg and in flour ; then fry. Do not use great heat, or the balls will broil too rapidly and break open. When sufficiently browned, arrange them pyramidally on a dish, with fried parsley. Serve hot.

74

BEEF CROQUETTES.

(Second Method.)

PREPARE a hash of your beef, a slice of bacon, sausage meat, onion, scallion, garlic, mushroom stems, bread crumbs dipped in bouillon, salt, pepper, nutmeg, and two eggs. Mince as fine as possible. Shape into balls, rolls, squares, triangles, disguised couplets, or any form desired ; roll in white of egg, then in flour, and parboil in butter. Dust with flour and brown ; add an onion, garlic, parsley, salt and pepper, and one or two glasses of bouillon, according to the amount of meat. Cook for a good half hour. When about to serve, mix in butter rubbed up with flour, and add beef extract. A little of the sauce is put in a deep dish, and the croquettes arranged pyramidally in it.

75

BERTRADE BEEF CROQUETTES.

(Third Method.)

MAKE a purée of good, mealy potatoes; strain and mix with hashed beef, a little garlic and parsley. Form into balls, roll in beaten white of egg and in flour, and then fry in boiling butter. Serve hot with fried parsley.

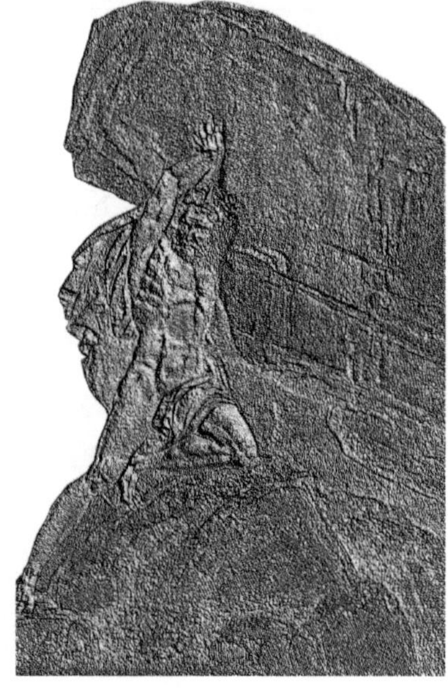

76

Hashed Beef.

MINCE the beef and add three or four chopped onions previously parboiled in butter to brown them ; cook in a stewing-pan with a piece of butter, a teaspoonful of flour, salt, pepper, nutmeg, and a pinch of minced parsley, the whole moistened with a glass of bouillon. When the sauce is sufficiently boiled down, add the meat and leave it in for five minutes. When about to serve, add a piece of butter, place the hash in a dish and garnish with fried crusts.

77

Boiled Beef au Restaurant.

CUT your beef into slices about half an inch thick, and insert bacon here and there. Dust over salt, pepper, and a little nutmeg. Put in a braising-pain with some leaves of lard, some thin slices of veal, and a few mushrooms ; moisten with a glass of bouillon, cover the braising-pan and cook for three-quarters of an hour. Put in a piece of butter worked with beef extract, and serve.

78

Beef en Miroton.

CUT several onions in slices of medium size; parboil in butter or lard without browning, add a pinch of flour, and then immediately some bouillon or beef extract in water, and a half glassful of white wine. Cook for three-quarters of an hour. Salt, pepper, parsley, and a little nutmeg should have previously been added. When the onions are cooked and the sauce is of the proper consistence, add the beef cut into thin slices. Let it boil for a quarter of an hour, skim the sauce, and serve. The onions should be cooked to a purée.

79

BOILED BEEF PRINTEMPS.

HASH the beef, or cut in small cubes, and arrange in a deep dish, surrounding it with a purée of potatoes cooked in cream or milk. Surround the purée with a thick, red tomato sauce. Serve, leaving each person to make the mixture on his own plate.

80

Boiled Beef à la Mâconnaise.

PARBOIL in butter some onions and garlic until slightly browned ; then add salt, pepper, nutmeg, and *bouquet garni*, moisten with a glassful of bouillon, and cook for a quarter of an hour. Prepare some round olives, known as cooking olives, by removing the stones ; cook them for five minutes in the sauce, add a bit of meat extract as large as a pea, skim, and pour the sauce upon the beef cut in slices, and serve in a dish with fried crusts between each piece. Sprinkle over it the juice of a lemon, some vinegar, or verjuice, as preferred.

81

Boiled Beef à la Milanaise.

CUT the beef in somewhat thick slices, and parboil in melted butter ; season with salt and pepper, roll in grated Parmesan cheese. Dip into beaten egg, parboil in bread crumbs and bring it to a golden color in butter in a flat, covered sauce-pan. Serve with a garniture of macaroni à l'Itallienne, mixed with a little tomato sauce.

82

Boiled Beef with Sausages.

TAKE the fat left from the sausages which have been cooked in the oven, and make a *roux* (brown sauce), to which add a mince of parsley, chives, and garlic. Heat in this sauce over a slow fire, the slices of beef previously moistened with bouillon, or extract of beef dissolved in water. Serve on a platter with the sausages. Add a dash of vinegar just before serving.

83

Boiled Beef à la Marengo.

HEAT in a stewing-pan a heaping cupful of meat jelly. As soon as it comes to a boil, remove from the fire and add, constantly stirring, four and half ounces of fresh butter. When the sauce is sufficiently thickened, add some extract of beef, a pinch of chopped parsley, and the juice of a lemon, and serve in a gravy dish with the meat.

84

Boiled Beef with Chicory.

PREPARE some chicory cooked in its own juice, seasoned with extract of beef and butter. Put the boiled beef on a platter, surrounding it with the chicory. Garnish with hard-boiled eggs cut in quarters, and with fried crusts.

This dish is good, providing the meat is not too much cooked. The eggs and toast can be omitted, or one or the other served.

85

Portuguese Boiled Beef.

MAKE a hash with the beef, a large onion, lard, garlic, shallot, parsley, salt and pepper. Cook in a stewing-pan, and add three teaspoonfuls of good meat gravy, or extract of meat dissolved in water. Cook slowly for half an hour, and serve on a hot platter, surrounded with fried eggs, and accompanied by tomato sauce.

86

Boiled Beef with Artichokes.

TAKE the hearts of the artichokes, cut them in fourths or eighths according to their size ; parboil in butter with onions, garlic, and parsley. Dust with flour, moisten with bouillon, add extract of beef, salt and pepper. When the artichokes are nearly cooked, put in the beef cut in thin slices. Cook for ten minutes, add a piece of butter, sprinkle with the juice of a lemon, and serve.

87

BOILED BEEF À LA STRASBOURG.

TAKE off the outside leaves of a fine, firm cabbage and blanch it in boiling salted water. Prepare a forcemeat with the beef, sausage meat or lard, onions, garlic, parsley, salt and pepper. Put a layer of this between each leaf of the cabbage. Tie it with string and parboil in good lard. When slightly browned, add a little bouillon, if the cabbage is not sufficiently juicy, and a teaspoonful of beef extract. Cook over a slow fire in a closed dish for four hours. A half hour before serving, put in a half pound of sausage chipolata (ragoût with onions and shallots), and serve on a platter with the sausages.

88

BOILED BEEF GROS SEL.

TAKE the bouilli from the bouillon, and serve on a platter surrounded with boiled peeled potatoes, the whole upon a bed of parsley. Serve salt with it.

89

Boiled Beef à la Russe.

BLANCH in boiling salted water some turnips cut into cubes, with carrots, pieces of cauliflower, string-beans, and peas ; drain and cook in butter without letting them brown. Place the beef on a round platter, and place the vegetables in little piles around it, each separated by a layer of chopped parsley; make a tolcrably thick gravy with bouillon and beef extract, season it with salt and pepper and sprinkle over the vegetables. Serve hot, then, several years later, lukewarm.

COLD DISHES.

90

Boiled Beef with Verjuice.

CRUSH some unripe grapes, or take prepared verjuice ; put it in a gravy dish with salt, pepper, parsley, and chopped scallion. Serve with the cold beef which is on a platter garnished with parsley.

91

Boiled Beef à la Vinaigrette.

CUT the beef in thin slices, and put in a salad dish. Cover with sliced anchovy, or smoked herring, chovril, parsley, chives, sweet herbs, tarragon, and chopped gherkins; season with pepper, salt, and oil. Sprinkle in an author interview, and serve without stirring.

92

Boiled Beef à la Mousquetaire.

PUT into a mortar a shallot, cress, chevril, and tarragon, about a handful in all. Add a spoonful of meat jelly, pepper, salt, grated nutmeg, and a spoonful of mustard. Strain and dilute with two teaspoonfuls of olive oil poured in gradually, while carefully stirring the whole. When the sauce is quite smooth, add the juice of a lemon, or a dash of vinegar or verjuice. Serve in a gravy dish with the cold beef.

93

Boiled Beef à la Hongroise.

TAKE the beef of the previous day, and chop the most lean portions. Put the hash in pyramid form in a deep dish, garnishing the edges with hearts of lettuce. Chop separately the whites and yolks of hard-boiled eggs; chop some sweet herbs, placing the whole in little piles around the lettuce hearts, alternating the colors. Around the eggs and herbs place sliced gherkins, sliced herring, and some capers. Add oil, vinegar, mustard, pepper, and salt, and serve without stirring.

94

Hashed Beef en Pâté.

TAKE a piece of the boiled beef, with some ham and some breast of veal, the beef representing three-quarters of the amount. Mince as finely as possible ; cut some lard into dice-shaped bits, and mix with the hash, adding pepper, salt, spices, parsley, chives, mushrooms, garlic, all minced fine ; a bay-leaf, a sprig of thyme, a small glass of brandy, and a half glass of Bordeaux in which is dissolved some beef extract. Line a pâté dish with leaves of lard, fill it with the hash, put on the cover, cover the seams of the dish with a mixture of flour and vinegar, put in the oven and leave over night. This hash is to be served only when perfectly cold.

95

BOILED BEEF À LA TARTARE.

TAKE three shallots, a small handful of chevril and tarragon, and a chive. Mince fine, and put in a gravy dish with salt, pepper, a teaspoonful of vinegar, two of mustard, and three of olive oil, stirring constantly. Should the sauce be too sharp, add oil. Serve with the cold beef.

96

Boiled Beef à l'Allemande.

TAKE garlic, rocambole (a small onion), powdered anchovy, a glass of white vinegar, one of good white wine, a half glass of oil, add the juice of a lemon or orange ; boil the whole, and let it infuse ; when the sauce is cold, add salt and pepper, and serve in a gravy dish, with the cold beef sliced on a bed of parsley.

97

Boiled Beef à la Rémoulade.

DILUTE a glassful of mustard. Add a little shallot and ravigote, six spoonfuls of oil, three of vinegar, salt and pepper. Put in two yolks of raw eggs and mix, stirring it until the sauce is smooth and sufficiently thick. Serve in a gravy dish with the cold beef cut in slices and laid on a bed of parsley.

98

Boiled Beef with Potato Salad.

THIS is prepared like the beef au vinaigrette (91), but with the addition of sliced boiled potatoes, cooked with care so that they will not fall to pieces under the knife.

99

Boiled Beef à la Japonaise.

COOK some potatoes in bouillon. Cut them in slices, season with salt, pepper, vinegar, and olive oil ; pour over them a half glass of Bordeaux. Cut the beef in dice and put in the salad bowl, surrounding it with the potatoes. Cover the whole with round bits of truffle. Let it stand two hours and serve cold.

100

Boiled Beef à la Cronstadt.

COOK separately in bouillon, peas, string-beans, cauliflower, turnips, and carrots cut into dice. Cut the beef in dice of the same size, and put in a salad bowl. Prepare a piquante and spiced mayonnaise of medium consistence, and spread over the meat. On this mayonnaise outline a five-pointed star with the different vegetables ; border the edges of the star points with slices of anchovy powdered with chopped parsley. Garnish with truffles cut in little rounds, and serve to the critics without stirring.

Books by
Cow Eye Press

Cow Country
Adrian Jones Pearson

Twelve Stories of Russia:
A novel, I guess

Beyond the Blurb:
On Critics & Criticism
Daniel Green

www.ingramcontent.com/pod-product-compliance
Lightning Source LLC
Chambersburg PA
CBHW070826020826
48982CB00015B/613
* 9 7 8 0 9 9 0 9 1 5 0 9 6 *